Printed by CreateSpace (an amazon.com company) and available at amazon.com and other retail outlets.

Nancy The Giraffe Finds Her Purpose

Jimmy The Turtle Conquers Fear

Lucy The Goose Learns To Listen

Three Complete Books by: **Treasa Snowman**
Illustrated by: **Ted Brennan**

Nancy The Giraffe
Finds Her Purpose

Written by: **Treasa Snowman**
Illustrated by: **Ted Brennan**

There once was a giraffe named Nancy who didn't like herself very much.

She would watch the lions and hear their roar and think, "Wow! They are so beautiful and so strong! I wish I could be a lion."

Then she would watch the elephants, and think "they do so much. They carry the people and all their important stuff." They serve such a tremendous purpose and help so many. I wish I could be an elephant.

Nancy was so busy wanting to be someone else, she really didn't get to know herself.

All she knew was that she wasn't beautiful, strong and brave like the lions.

She wasn't useful and needed like the elephants.

Nancy really was sad most of the time, wondering why God made her a giraffe.

Maybe He had made a mistake.

Nancy didn't have many friends; she usually kept her distance from all the other animals. She never felt like she belonged. It wasn't that they were mean, it was just that she really didn't believe she was worthy or welcome.

One day, as she was watching the beautiful flamingos do a dance wishing she could be beautiful and dance too, she overheard them talking to each other. "We are praying and dancing to ask our Lord Jesus to please make it rain."

You see, Nancy didn't know the other animals were starving because of drought. She was so involved with her own self-pity she hadn't even noticed the other animals had no food.

Nancy cried out to Jesus, "If You are real, change me, help me to like myself and love others enough to help when they are in need.

I want to be used by You, Lord, but I am just a giraffe."
"Just a giraffe?" God replied.
"Nancy, you are fearfully and wonderfully made, and I have a purpose for your life." Then God told Nancy to pick the leaves from the tops of the trees to feed the other animals. So Nancy did.

The other animals couldn't reach them and were starving. So God used Nancy to save the animals!

God will use you to save others in a very different way. Tell others about Jesus and pray this prayer with them so they can be saved and have eternal life with Jesus!

"Dear Jesus, I believe in You. I believe You died on the cross and rose again 3 days later to save sinners like me. Come into my heart and change my life today! In Jesus' name, Amen."

If you just prayed this prayer with someone you helped JESUS save someone. Yeah!

Jimmy The Turtle
Conquers Fear

Written by: **Treasa Snowman**
Illustrated by: **Ted Brennan**

There once was a turtle named Jimmy. Every time anything at all happened he would hide in his shell.

While the other turtles would swim and play, Jimmy would lay in the grass. He was afraid of water, so he would just watch.

When the other turtles would have races with their friends the rabbit, the squirrel, the fox, and sometimes other animals, Jimmy would hide in his shell afraid of all the other animals.

No one invited Jimmy to play anymore because he was such a bore. He spent the whole time in his shell.

Jimmy became very lonely and afraid. He almost never came out of his shell.

One day Jimmy cried out,
"God, if you are real, make
me not afraid!"

The next day Jimmy was in
his shell when he heard a
yell for
help!
It was
Robin
the frog.

She was in the water stuck
between two logs.

Jimmy looked around.
There was no one!
He couldn't just let his
friend Robin drown. He
was afraid, so he prayed
"Jesus, please help me to
be brave!" Jimmy jumped
in and moved the log so
Robin could swim free.

Exhausted and tired, she jumped on Jimmy's back and he swam her to shore.

From then on Jimmy wasn't afraid. He knew he had Jesus by his side!

Jimmy even started his own business giving small animals rides on his shell down the river, or to the other side.

Jimmy is rarely in his shell anymore and gets invited to everything. He has a lot of friends and feels love because he doesn't let fear stop him anymore.

Lucy The Goose
Learns To Listen

Written by: **Treasa Snowman**
Illustrated by: **Ted Brennan**

There once was a goose named Lucy. Lucy was very loud and always talked about herself, her problems, and her dreams.

Whenever someone would start to talk she would always change the subject back to herself.

Most of her friends didn't like to hang out with her for very long, because they never got to talk. They thought Lucy just didn't care about them. Lucy wondered what she had done wrong.

"Why doesn't anyone want to hang out with me except for Neva?" she asked herself.
(Neva was a deaf duck, she could not hear.)

Even though Neva was deaf,
she could read lips and
knew what Lucy was upset
about. Neva explained to
Lucy that
her friends
were
upset
because

she never let them talk.
They thought she only cared
about herself.

Lucy didn't understand. She never meant to hurt anyone. She was just always talking; not even knowing her words might hurt others. It was just talk, talk, talk!

Lucy prayed, "Jesus, why do I do this?

Please help me to change."

Jesus showed Lucy that as a gosling (a baby goose) she never got any attention.

That hurt, so she learned to get attention by talking about herself all the time.

Jesus told Lucy that He loves her, He always has and always will. She learned that His love is enough. Now she doesn't feel like she has to bring attention to herself any more.

Lucy and Neva planned a big party and all their friends came. Lucy listened to their stories that day and learned a lot of things she didn't know about her friends.

For example, Noreen, who was a beautiful peacock, had just lost her dad, which was really sad. Lucy didn't even know about this because she was always talking.

She learned about Jimmy
the turtle who was always
afraid and had conquered
fear with Jesus' help.

As her friends talked all night, Lucy learned so much she didn't know and felt closer than ever to her friends. They knew her and all her stories, now she knew theirs.

After everybody left, Lucy thanked Jesus for showing her that talking is ok, but everyone needs a turn. And Jesus reminded her that He loves and adores her and she will never be ignored!

The Bible says that we are "fearfully and wonderfully made" by God and He loves us and adores us!

Treasa L. Snowman

was born in 1969 in Waverly, New York. She moved to Florida in her youth where she lived until her adult life. As a child, she struggled with fear, insecurity, and her identity. As an adult, she moved back north with her family. She began attending His Tabernacle Family Church in Horseheads, NY where she became a Sunday School teacher and noticed the same fear and insecurities in the children that she had experienced. God inspired her to get back to her first love, which is writing, and He gave her creative ideas for children's books.

God used many people at His Tabernacle Family Church to make this dream a reality. All Glory be to God! And many thanks to all the people Jesus used to make this happen! Special thanks to Ted Brennan who illustrated and made the story come to life!

Made in the USA
Middletown, DE
12 December 2017